Stephanie Blake

I don't want to go to school

GECKO PRESS

There was once
a
cheeky
little
rabbit.

You might know him already.

When his mother told him,
"Simon, tomorrow is your
first day at school!"
he replied,
"I'm not going!"

When his father said,
"But, my little rabbit,
you'll learn the alphabet,"
Simon replied,
"I'm not going!"

That night,
Simon
couldn't
sleep…

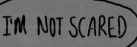

"MUMMY!"

**"I DON'T WANT
TO GO
TO SCHOOL!"**

His mother said,
"But you're the
bravest
little rabbit
in the world.
You're my super-rabbit."

Simon replied,
"I'm not going!"

Next morning,
when his mother said,
"Hurry up and eat your toast,
my little rabbit.
It's almost time to go to school,"
he replied,
"I'm not going!"

When they walked to school
and his father said,
"Don't worry,
you'll make friends
and learn lots of new things.
You're my **BIG BRAVE** bunny,"
Simon replied,
"I'm not going!"

**Outside school,
when Dad hugged his**
little
**rabbit
and said,
"See you later, Simon.
I'm going now,"
Simon replied
in a**
tiny,
tiny,
little voice,
"Not going!"

**At school
he did
hundreds
of things.**

First of all, he cried.

Then he did a drawing.

Then he played.

Then he ate chocolate mousse.

Then he had a rest.

In the afternoon, he did some drumming.

At three o'clock,
when his mother came and said,
"It's time to go home now,
my little rabbit,"
Simon replied,

"I'm not going!"